THE CIRCUS

by Lindsey Michael Miller   Illustrated by Phillip Griswold

Hickory Tales Publishing LLC
Bowling Green, Kentucky 2005

THE CIRCUS

First Edition
Published March 2005 by Hickory Tales Publishing LLC
841 Newberry St., Bowling Green, Kentucky 42103
Printed in China

ISBN 0-9709104-8-7

Library of Congress Card Catalog Number 2004118312

Dedication
This book is dedicated to the exploration of imagination, creativity, and inspiration

"The circus! The circus! What great fun we'd have.
　　All the clowns and the acrobats! Can we go, Dad?"

"Well I don't know, kids. Are you ready to see?"
　　The dad asked slowly smiling—his kids filled with glee.

"All those puppets, and walkers of high-wired beams,
　　All the people in stupor, entranced by the scenes
Of the elephants standing all tall in a row,
　　Or the twelve fingered lady with twelve painted toes?"

"Oh, yes, Dad! Oh, yes!" Said the first of his kids.
Jake was dreaming of visions with tightly closed lids.

"I am ready to see all the things just like these:
Like the great flying men on the swinging trapeze,
Or the tricky horse riders who ride with such care
On the backs of their horses and ride sitting bare.
And forget not those tigers that scare with their roar,
Or the monkeys who make you clap yelling, 'Encore!'"

In reply to his thought his bro, Thomas, did speak.
And he said enough good things to last them a week.
"Let us not forget, Jake, the ring master's part.
For without him the circus would just fall apart.
Or the way that he calls all the people to look
At the little clown car and the clowns that it took

To the center attraction, where all of them fell
   In such humorous fashion, and no one could tell
      If those clowns in the car were done taking the dive.
         Counting one, two, three, four, and perhaps even five.

But before Tom could say more, his sister chimed in
'Cause cute Jessica thought it not rude or a sin.

"Exciting! Exciting! To watch and to taste
All the dozens of foods there that won't go to waste.
Like the popcorn, and snow cones, and elephant ears,
And the ice cream with toppings that last you for years,
And the pink cotton candy that makes your hands stick,
Or the bright caramel apples, which always will drip,

And the bright-green, exciting, great Popsicle tray
With its millions of Popsicles there on display,
Showing all different colors, shapes, sizes, and molds,
With their eye-catching names written big and in bold,
Such as Zingers, and Rockets, and Blue-Bellied Bears,
And the Fiery Wowwies, and Red-Colored Flares.
Next to Slimy Sea Snakes, which come red, green, or blue,
Or the Choco-Pop-Sockos, Green Grabbers, Kazoos,
Siding Splitters, Cute Critters, and Red Throwing Darts,
Or the Double-With-Trouble, which comes in two parts.

But the counting's not over; count six and then seven,
And then for amazement come ten and eleven,
Twelve, thirteen, and fourteen. How can there be more?
And they all look so funny, it just makes me roar!"

Naming only a few from the Popsicle stand.
There are way, way too many to count on your hand."

"That's right kids! That's right! I remember them all,
'Cause when I was just your age, I had such a ball!
With that music so boomingly played by the band
As they sat, dressed in red, in the far seated stands.

And the tuba man played all the low sounding notes,
He, the biggest and widest of all the band blokes.
    With his face ever cherry and quite a bit round,
    One could say that he looks like his instrument sounds.
        So the top of the band sat the tuba man there,
        Just below him the trombonists rested their rears.
            Being numbered in three, sitting straight in a row,
            Sat the trombonists playing, and boy did they blow!
                Pushing forth, pulling back, blowing tune after tune,
                You would think that they would be quite good with harpoons.
                    And on that note I'll say that they looked like they'd hit
                    Those four trumpeters, sitting below in the pit.
    Oh, the trumpets! My gosh! I had almost forgot
    That the trumpeters played in the musical pot.
        Being smaller and thinner, yes, lesser in stout,
        Never did make them lesser, but greater in count.
            And they blew their brass trumpets as loud as they pleased.
            For the high notes were needed, the greatest of these.
                Are there any band instruments that I have not famed?
    Oh, the flutes, and the xylophones have not yet been named.
            And the organist playing through shiny, gold pipes,
                Or the bells that can come in three sizes and types.

But the funniest sighting is yet still to come,
For what hasn't been mentioned are men and their drums.
Which us baffle because they do not play the part
That one thinks that they ought, if one thinks he's smart.
Yes, the biggest of drums with its big padded mallets
Is played by the smallest of men in the ballad.

In fact, so it seems to the visible eye
That this drum has encompassed the poor little guy.
And if that's not all, just wait, and you'll see.
On the biggest of men, with the biggest of knees,
Sits the smallest of drums colored red and bright yellow.
This drum can't be seen on the big, brawny fellow.
It looks, to the eye, as he lets his arms fly,
That there's nothing he's hitting, just open blue sky.

All the rest of the men, sitting next to those two
Do appear just as strange as these first two men do,

Like the tympani player whose hair is so thick
  And so long that I'm shocked he can pound out a lick
    On those drums that he plays, for his hair covers all.
      It's a miracle he can see through that dense wall.
Or the man who plays cymbals who's thin and quite high

Looks compressed like his cymbals, I'd say, by and by.
But the comical thing, to this man, happens when
He picks up his two cymbals, and crashes and then
He vibrates like they do. Oh, it's such a sight
When he tries to stop shaking with all of his might."

"How great, Dad! How great! You have told it so well,"
Said his daughter, sweet Jenny. Much more she could tell.
"What a great big, red band, I can see it all now,
With their suits and their flutes. But I want to know how
Those fast motorbikes ride through the big metal ball.
For they start with just one, and he seems like he'll fall.
But he doesn't; he circles around and around.
So impossibly fast that I wait for the sound,
As I close my small eyes and just wait for the crowd
To stop clapping, because they are cheering so loud.
But that man never falls, but in fact, to my shock,
He is joined by three more, before closing the lock.
And they spin and they twist and they turn and they weave
But they never do touch. I can hardly believe,
Such a sight with my eyes, though I've seen magic acts.
'Cause these cycles play tricks with what seems to be facts."

"Oh, magic you said, I remember, what fame,"
Did cute Jessica say, interrupting again.

"Oh, the man of great magic who stood in the ring
With his ladies, at beckon, such things they would bring,
Like the box with the lady he'd cut into two,
Or the trick hoop he'd turn into purple or blue,
Or the handkerchiefs suddenly turning to birds.
I was so much amazed I had hardly a word!

But the singly most shocking of all his fun
Was that somehow he'd gotten my hot dog and bun,
Swiped it right from my mouth, as I was taking a bite
And then abra kadabra he had it in flight
And then into his hand he'd extended quite high.
All the people were clapping, but I could just cry,
'Cause I wanted my hot dog, I wanted it back
But he ate it, that fiend; I should give him a whack!"

There she stopped for her face started turning quite red,
So her brother, small Thomas, spoke his thoughts instead:
  "The magic was great, but it's making me tire.
  The best part for me was the man who blew fire.
    This man was so cool with his hat that was big,
    And his pants that were bigger, and his face like a pig,
      With his shiny blue sash, and his pointy green shoes,
      And his red, puffy pants and his turban in blues.
        Such cool stuff he could do, as he walked though the tent!
        He blew fire at people, and people he sent
          Up the stairs. They were running, and screaming in fear.
          And as they were running, they swore they could hear
            His great laughter, his chuckle. He knew that he'd learned
            How to blow his great fire and leave them unburned."

"No, that part is stupid!" Said Jen in reply.
Said so rudely that Thomas thought that she should die.
"I think that the act that is coolest, not fire,
The woman who daringly walks the tight wire.
Who's dressed like a bird, with a feathery cap
And a great, giant feather attached to her back.
She's so graceful when walking, and balancing well.
You don't even think about 'what if she fell.'
But then that's not all; there's more that I love
When I'm looking upon this sweet, rope-walking dove.
She does spins, and back flips, all more to surprise
That she fearlessly does them, not op'ning her eyes."

Oh, yeah! Well, you're wrong!" Said Jake to his sis.
"I have one that's better I've placed on my list.
The sign says it all, if it needs to be said,
On the side of the cannon, it's big and in red.

And it clearly states well it's the best of the acts.
"Great Devil of Dares," it says quite in fact.
But the best part he does when he gets in the gun.
They just shoot him so high, and it looks very fun.

So you see now that mine is much better than yours."
And with that statement said, they broke out into wars.

All the kids grabbed a hand or a face or some hair,
Or a jacket or shirt. They did not fight so fair.

They were kicking and screaming and shouting and then
They were fighting until their smart dad had a plan.

"Now kids," said their dad, "I want you to stop now!
    Or we'll stay in this house. Stop having a cow!
We'll not go to the circus, and you'll stay and do chores!
    You'll all sweep and vacuum and mop up the floors!"

At that they stopped fighting and looked up at him,
    And said very urgently in unison,
"Let's go Dad! Let's go!" Cried the kids to their dad.
    Let's stop talking and go, or we'll miss it and be sad."

So they got in their car and drove down past the tree
  Where the paper had said that the circus would be,
Past the bridge, and the park, and the zoo to the grounds
  Where the tents were set up. And they drove right around
To the place where you park, and behold what they saw
  Was far greater than their dreams, and they sat with dropped jaw.
As they watched the circus take place, with the lions and the bears
  They did nothing but sit on the benches and stare

At the elephants, tigers, and monkeys, and birds
  And the ring master, and clowns dressed too funny for words,
And the Popsicles, apples, and caramel pops,
  And the motorbikes, fireman, and trapeze on top,
Or the ropewalker, daredevil, magic man's wand,
And the strong man whose muscles must really be strong,
  And the dogs on the little blue bikes that they rode,
And the band that was better than even Dad had retold.

And they saw much, much more, than they thought that they would,
So their trip to the circus had been very, very good.

The Circus is the first in a series of books by children's author, Lindsey Miller, and incorporates the outstanding artwork of illustrator, Phil Griswold. We are indebted to them both for their contribution to this book.

Lindsey Michael Miller lives and works as an author and freelance journalist in Denver, Colorado. He spends much of his time with his parents and younger siblings, who live in Colorado Springs, Colorado. Besides writing he spends his time snowboarding, rock climbing, mountain biking, dancing and dating cute girls. He plans to pursue other books, both for adults and children, as well as to go on to Graduate School for another degree in Creative Writing.

Phillip Griswold is a freelance illustrator and artist. He received his B.F.A. from Oral Roberts University in Tulsa, Oklahoma and he lives and works in his native New England. He has painted and drawn portraits by commision, but also enjoys creation of artwork from his own imagination. This is his first children's book.

Children, as well as adults, are discussing the new fantasy series of Prince Albert books, full of magical adventure, by Brian Daffern. The first three books are *Prince Albert in a Can*, *Prince Albert, Book 2: The Beast School* and *Prince Albert, Book 3: The Realm Pirates*, all available at, or on order, from your local bookstore.

Or you may qualify for free postage by ordering at our website:
http://www.hickorytales.com

For older children and adults we have *Hoot Owl Shares the Dawn* by Jennifer French and *The Promise* by Charles Entwistle.

For teenagers and adult adventurers, we offer *Quicksilver Deep* by Buddy Cox, *Chalmette: The Battle for New Orleans and How the British Nearly Stole the Louisiana Territory* by Charles Patton, and the exciting outdoor challenges of *BearClaw* by Ron Schaaf.